My friend Sleep

Laura Baker Hannah Peck

words & pictures

When night-time falls, a gentle darkness fills my room.

It flits and floats, then rests softly over me.

I snuggle deep down into bed and let my eyes slide shut...

My friend
Sleep

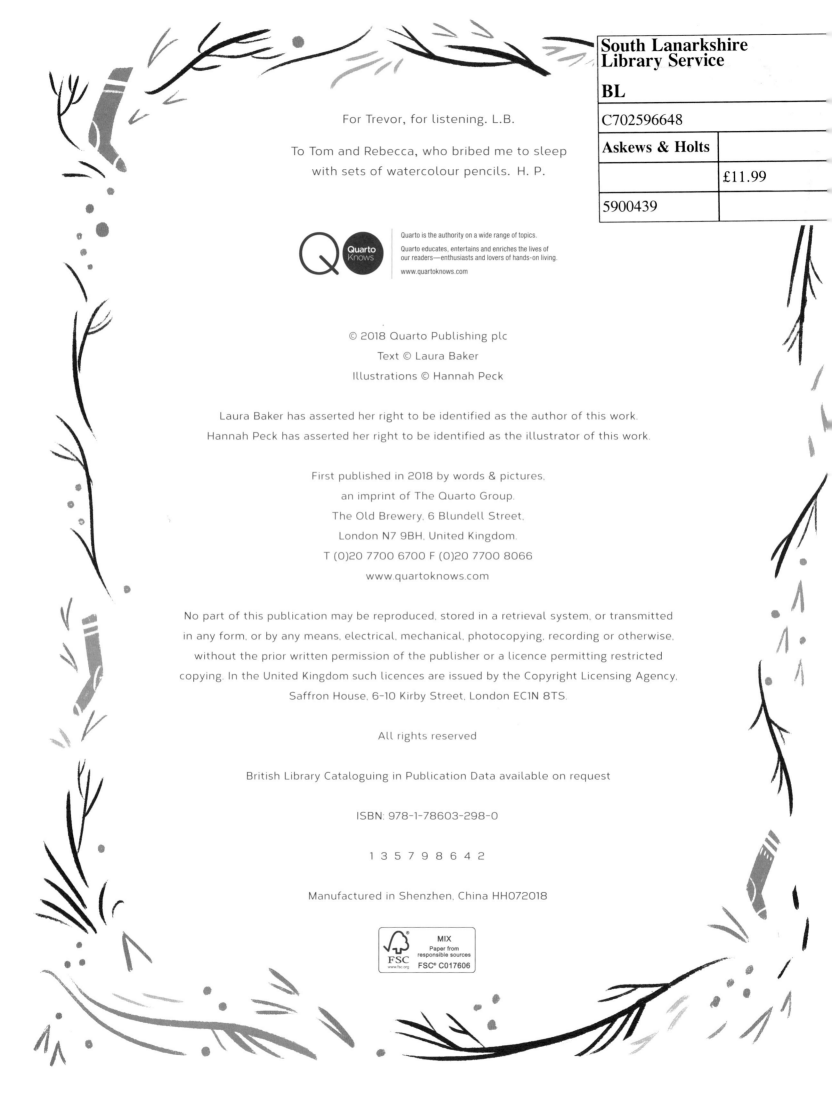

For Trevor, for listening. L.B.

To Tom and Rebecca, who bribed me to sleep
with sets of watercolour pencils. H. P.

Quarto is the authority on a wide range of topics.
Quarto educates, entertains and enriches the lives of
our readers—enthusiasts and lovers of hands-on living.
www.quartoknows.com

© 2018 Quarto Publishing plc
Text © Laura Baker
Illustrations © Hannah Peck

Laura Baker has asserted her right to be identified as the author of this work.
Hannah Peck has asserted her right to be identified as the illustrator of this work.

First published in 2018 by words & pictures,
an imprint of The Quarto Group.
The Old Brewery, 6 Blundell Street,
London N7 9BH, United Kingdom.
T (0)20 7700 6700 F (0)20 7700 8066
www.quartoknows.com

British Library Cataloguing in Publication Data available on request

ISBN: 978-1-78603-298-0

1 3 5 7 9 8 6 4 2

Manufactured in Shenzhen, China HH072018

MIX
Paper from
responsible sources
FSC® C017606
FSC
www.fsc.org

That's when
my friend *Sleep*
comes to play.

Sleep sings into my ear,
and in my slumber I can hear,
"Come with me, my friend, take hold of my hand.
Together we'll travel through night's dreamland."

Sleep shows me things I never see in the day.
Some good, some not-so-good.

But Sleep is always by my side as we explore new wonders of the night.

Tonight, *Sleep* takes me to a magical land bursting with delicious sweets and scrumptious treats.

Candyfloss clouds hover above delights that stretch as far as the horizon.

Sleep and I grin at each other as we run
to try every mouth-watering morsel.

Ice cream sundaes
with sparkling sprinkles...

crystal jellies that
glint and glisten...

and plump, dewy berries
that fill our noses with
the most irresistible scent.

We fill our tummies to full, then Sleep sings again,

"Come with me, my friend, take hold of my hand.
Together we'll travel through night's dreamland."

The sweets and treats sweep open like grand gates, inviting us into a land of dinosaurs and trains and a fair of fun.

A helter-skelter swirls while teacups twirl...

And then I see it: the biggest Big Wheel in the world!

We hop on board and soar up, up, up, into the sky.

We feed leaves to the dinosaurs in the trees,

then higher still we climb and climb.

I squeeze *Sleep*'s hand, and *Sleep* squeezes mine.

Aliens bip and bop in alien code.
Somehow we know they are
saying hello, so back we
shout, "Hello, hello, hello!"

Suddenly, something bright
and fiery comes curling,
twisting, curving around
the planets and stars.
A dragon!

The Big Wheel reaches
its highest point, and
Sleep calls out, "JUMP!"

With a giant leap, we jump straight
onto the creature's back.

Into the air, faster and faster,
Sleep and me. "Whee!"

Through the clouds we fly, soaring,

swerving, loop-the-looping.

But then, the dragon drops us off
at a gloomy cave and Sleep sings softly,
"Come with me, my friend,
take hold of my hand.
Together we'll travel
through night's dreamland."

I hide behind *Sleep* as we peep
and peer into darkness.
A shiver darts through me.
Sometimes *Sleep* takes me
to places that scare me a little.

Suddenly, a monster bursts out.
"BOO!" It towers over us with
a menacing monster shadow.

I start to run, but, ever so gently,
Sleep reaches for my hand
and sings again,
"Come with me, my friend,
take hold of my hand.
Together we'll face
what's in night's dreamland."

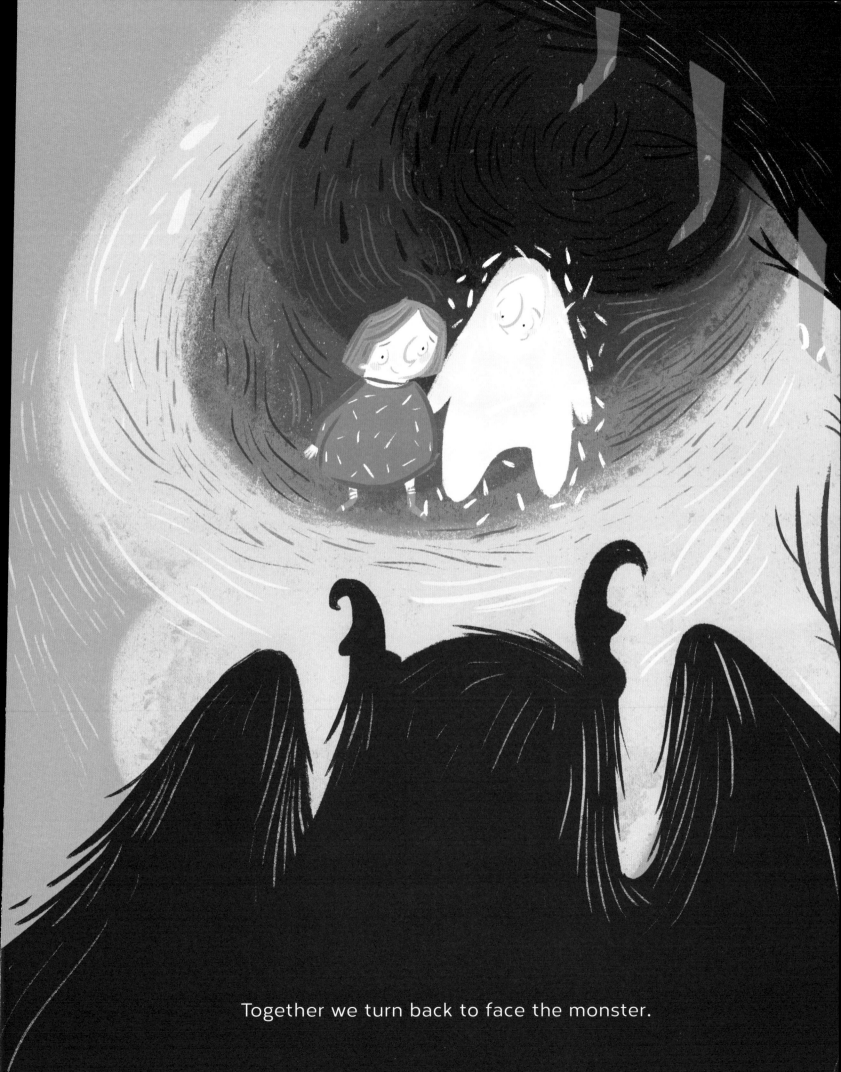

Together we turn back to face the monster.

Sleep hands me a magic wand.
I swish and sway the wand through
the air, singing:

"Swirl, twirl... In my dreams,
everything's not what it seems!"

The monster shrinks – down, down,
down – to the size of a dog.
His claws turn to paws, and his jaws
turn into a warm smile.

I stroke his head. "You're not
so scary after all," I say.

Sleep tickles behind
the monster's ears.

Then my friend $Sleep$ holds out a hand one last time, and I take it gently.

Together we fly back to bed through the night sky, leaving a soft trail of stars behind us.

"Goodbye, *Sleep*," I whisper.

"See you for more adventures tonight."

In the morning light, I wake with a smile.

I hop from my bed and spread my arms wide.

Then I swoop and soar through my room
on a memory of dreams, ready for
the wonders of another day.